Praise for Constance Debré

'Challenging yet empowering .
Times

'At once cavernous and concise
cool, and unbiased in its assessn
York Review of Books

'Shocking for its psychologically blank, bare-knuckle
swagger' *Telegraph*

'Ferocious emotional honesty … A bracing read and a
timely reminder that attitudes are often far slower to
change than legislation' *Irish Times*

'Committed to truth-telling, no matter how rough, but
also intriguingly suspended in a cloud of unknowing and
pain, *Love Me Tender* is a wry, original, agonizing book
destined to become a classic of its kind' Maggie Nelson,
author of *The Argonauts*

'Exhilarating' Eileen Myles, author of *Afterglow*

'Bold and brash and at the same time quietly controlled
… Debré is brilliantly deadpan' Chloë Ashby, *Spectator*

'Her scalpel-like stylistic approach makes the rebellious
content of Debré's novels resonate all the more' *Prospect*

'This is the most addictive book I've read since I can
remember… Debré's observations about how men see
women, and how she now sees women in turn, as a lesbi-
an, are brutal and revelatory. Read the earth-shatteringly
emotional *Love Me Tender* next, where Debré fights to
keep custody of her young son post-divorce, despite her
ex-husband's best efforts' *AnOther Magazine*

Offenses

Offenses

Constance Debré

**Translated by
Jeffrey Zuckerman**

Tuskar Rock Press

First published in Great Britain in 2026 by
Tuskar Rock Press,
an imprint of Profile Books Ltd
29 Cloth Fair
London
EC1A 7JQ

www.profilebooks.com

First published in the United States of America in 2026 by Semiotext(e)

Design: Hedi El Kholti

10 9 8 7 6 5 4 3 2 1

Printed and bound in Great Britain by
CPI Group (UK) Ltd, Croydon, CR0 4YY

A CIP catalogue record for this book is available from the British Library.

Our product safety representative in the EU is BGC Sustainability & Compliance, 7 avenue du Général Leclerc, Paris, 75014, France https://baldwinglobalconsulting.com

ISBN 978 1 80522 108 1
eISBN 978 1 80522 109 8

You walk over us, I don't know if you know that. No I think it's something you've forgotten. You live off of us, we are the price of what you are, you don't wonder. But you know each thing comes at a price, that that's how the world works.

The apartment is on the third floor, left side. It's a two-bedroom. The bedroom and the storage room have a view of the parking lot and the street. The other rooms, of behind the building. The bedroom is cluttered with clothes, things, old papers. The white PVC roller shade is pulled halfway down. The bed is made, the folded-up cover set at the end. In the next room, the storage room, are piled-up bags, suitcases, empty boxes. The kitchen has a gas stove, a freezer on top of the fridge, a Formica table. There's a mug and a pot in the sink. Plastic bags hang from a hook fastened to the wall. In the bathroom, buckets overflow with laundry. Everything in the sitting room is brown. The linoleum, the wallpaper, the furniture's plywood. An old-timey brown browned further by time, which seems to swallow up all other color. On the sideboard, black-and-white photos (a man in uniform, hat and shoulder cords, a woman, children in front of houses), an upside-down cup, two porcelain cat figurines, postcards, fake pink roses. To the right of the sideboard, an armchair. On the armchair, clothes. The table is in the middle of the room. It's draped with a blue-and-yellow patterned oilcloth and a red plastic placemat. It's covered with things. Letters, newspapers, a crossword digest, mineral water, pill bottles, a remote control, a glass, a Crédit Lyonnais card holder, some Hypermarché coupons, the business card for a rheumatologist mentioning two appointments with no month or year specified, Wednesday 22th Friday 24th. A pile of brochures lies strewn across the floor, one is a yellowing porn magazine, the prices are in francs. A chair is on its side.

She's on the floor to the left of the table laid out flat legs spread elbows on the floorboards hands on her chest. Her eyes are half shut her mouth is open her tongue is purple. She's wearing a pink bathrobe and a white floral night-gown. Her right foot is in a slipper the other one has ended up under the sideboard. The bathrobe is buttoned all the way to her navel, the nightgown reaches her waist. She's got an adult diaper on, she's old. Her upper body, from her head to her shoulders, is soaking in a puddle of blood. In a pool of blood. Thick clumpy dark blood spread out on the linoleum. A gaping wound runs from the base of her neck to her right cheek. Her right ear has a hearing aid in. A trickle of blood drips from her mouth, forks across the left cheek, one branch toward her ear the other toward her scalp. Her right cheek is covered in blood. She has other wounds, not as deep, on her neck her head her hands her torso her belly. She has ten wounds in all. In technical terms, her death is the result of a right cervical fracture from a stab wound with external bleeding from the wounds of the right jugular vein and the larynx.

Everything's a mess. Everything's born a mess and it's all downhill from there. Things beings everything's ugly keep that in mind. Keep that in mind if it's slipped your mind. I don't know how this came to be. As if this is how it's always been. As if this turns out to be everywhere, in the landscape the streets the things the sentences the living the dead. Maybe *ugly* isn't the word, maybe *useless absurd grotesque atrocious* is the word. Something that would be atrocious but isn't even so because it's insignificant. Something that would be useless if it weren't atrocious. Grotesque yes maybe, because fundamentally laughable. But feelings sentences words are saved up. Endured only to become like walls that break like dog parks that reek. Even our bodies are rotten, born sham. With me it's my kidneys and my ears. I got some treatment, there were three operations on my eardrums. That was the plan for my kidneys too, but now I don't know. We'll see about my missing teeth. In any case it is what it is. With my mother it's her kidneys too. And her soul after that. She's on meds, I've never known her off them, depression she says. She couldn't take care of us. My brothers and sister were put in foster care. I almost was, too, I wish I'd been. With my father it's his heart, although he isn't that old. Maybe his garbageman job's worn him down or maybe booze has. The old lady's body wasn't a pretty sight either. Maybe it's food, maybe it's all the ugliness around that ends up getting into our bodies. Thou shalt not kill but we will.

He asked if she needed him, she said no, he said he'd stop by anyway. When he came down she had the door open already. He started talking, she said that money-wise, *he* owed *her*, that every time he ran her errands he kept the change. Running her errands was how he knew her credit card PIN, that was how he got the idea. She'd done the math, she showed him the paper. She said it came out to thirty-four euros, that he had to pay her back or she'd talk to his father.

She started getting worked up, he raised his voice, she got even louder. He'd done what he'd come for, what he'd planned to. He grabbed the bag on the chair where it always was. She saw him, she grabbed his arm, he shoved her off, she fell. He tried to step over her to leave, she caught his ankle, she hung on. She was heavy, heavy with her old age with her being poor, heavy with her whole worthless life. She didn't let go. He was upright, standing with his whole thin self. She was the weight of things, a concrete block.

It's a trap of course it's a trap. You think he doesn't see that. Of course he sees that. That's all he sees, other people's trap his own trap. The trap isn't hidden, it's gaping. Traps are made for jumping right into. There are times when all that's left is to jump into the trap.

He grabbed the knife. The knife that was always there in front of her on the table like the bag that was always there on the chair near the window. There are things, we live in a world of things. For her it was her knife her table her *Télé 7 Jours* her always-on TV her pill bottles her adult diaper her cane her credit card for her worthless life with her worthless money. As worthless as his life as hash as the cité as his mother as being a bastard as wasting fifteen hours a day on his PlayStation whole afternoons hanging out at the stadium smoking with the others and the baby in the stroller.

He's feeling weird. All he remembers is the stab to the throat to make her quiet down because she was shouting and then blood, blood that wouldn't stop. How could he have thrust so deep into her throat, how could he have cut through her voice box while leaning over her with the small kitchen knife, the same one everybody has, the one every one of us has, that's what surprised them most. They suspected he was lying, that he'd cut her throat from behind while she was sitting at her table and he was standing. It was like he'd said, her on the ground and him on his knees, he killed her the way people pray. The angel was him.

She and he were good versus evil, but not like the cops the judges thought. The evil was this woman. This woman who was ugly, who was heavy, who held him back, everything that held him back. The evil was the weight of things the ugliness of everything. There did have to be a struggle. For once, once in life. To have fought, to have gone all the way, to have come face-to-face. For once, once for the rest of his life. Maybe at that point she was no longer the evil. Maybe that was what happened when he came down on her with the knife. That the evil passed from her to him. That he took the evil, the evil of her worthless life of her spitefulness of her ugliness. That he saved her, her and all the others, that he took on all the filth of that worthless life, her life and the lives of all those who'd been around him for so long, forever. Maybe that's what they're for, those people like them, maybe It's taking all the evil that murderers are for, to hell with damnation.

It's a trap of course it's a trap you think I don't see that of course I see that all I see is that there are times when all that's left is to jump into the trap.

Could nineteen still be young. He lives at his father's place with his girlfriend and their daughter. Soon she'll be three she was born when they were sixteen. They met at fifteen they moved in together fast. His father's place isn't big but it's better than his mother's because of the fights there. He doesn't work she doesn't either (they aren't students of course not) so they live at his father's place, a two-bedroom, here it's called an F3. It's the same as the old lady's, the downstairs neighbor, the one he killed this morning. He stabbed her ten times he left blood everywhere. Of course he was arrested several days later, all the evidence was there it wasn't hard, murder happens to make something stop. Is it possible for things to stop, for everything not to always be the same flat hue, the same tone, at the same speed that swallows you up, stifling, short of breath, sooner or later no oxygen left in the brain, is it possible for everyone to be quiet, the baby, his mother, the dealer, the cops, the judges, every one of them be quiet. They can do whatever they like with him, he'll give them his body, as long as he can be quiet, as they let him stop answering, leave him alone, that's all he wants, that's all he's ever wanted.

Maybe that's why he liked the old lady, yes, even loved, let him speak of love. Usually she didn't ask him questions didn't ask him about anything. That was why he helped her here and there ran her errands at the Carrefour at the pharmacy took her to physical therapy. Because they didn't talk to each other because she didn't ask him about anything. Because of that and the small euro bill she gave him but it wasn't much the euro bill was just so they'd believe this wasn't just being nice, being nice isn't a thing that would have been a whole mess, a small bill made sure that there wasn't anybody in a mess, that there weren't any questions why, the reason of effects as Pascal put it.

She had no visitors apart from the ones to help with errands and the podiatrist on Fridays. She couldn't walk well she couldn't see well she couldn't hear well. She was in her mid-eighties. Her only objects of value, so to speak, were her wedding ring and a pair of earrings. She'd always been poor. She'd been a widow for years. She had a spousal pension of some eight hundred euros. She hadn't really worked, apart from some housekeeping when she was on her own with children. She was born nearby. Her parents had a little house until it was seized so the highway could be built. She had been living in the building since it went up, since the sixties, the decade of buildings highways going up. She had three children. Two died. A daughter at six, a son at twenty-three. She didn't talk to her one son still alive anymore, he didn't talk to her anymore. When there was a knock she looked through the peephole, if she didn't recognize the face she didn't open up. She wasn't a member of any club, any group. Her only acquaintances now were for running errands. All she did was watch TV. Maybe she didn't care about anyone anymore. Maybe there's an age when people stop caring about others. She had a dog, it died long ago, there was a photo on the sideboard.

So did her son, a Yorkshire and a Jack Russell. One of the first to be questioned, long long before—even though it happened quickly—before the perp was arrested, he testified. That on Friday he had clocked in at eight, clocked out for lunch at noon, come home to eat with his wife, headed back to work, gone home around five, walked the dogs around seven, watched TV with his wife. That on Saturday just like every other Saturday he'd gone to the Leclerc with his wife, they'd come home for lunch, he'd had a nap, he'd stayed home, he'd walked the dogs, he'd watched TV. That on Sunday just like every other Sunday they'd gone to the market, come home for lunch he'd taken a nap, walked the dogs, watched TV. He'd seen his mother on the street on Thursday the night before the murder. She had her arm crutch and a shopping bag. They hadn't waved to each other. He wasn't sure how to spell his mother's maiden name. Her *nom de jeune fille* as the French put it no matter how long it's been since the women were young girls.

On the official police report were words like *unbearable vile headstrong mean difficult*. That's how they—the building manager the nurse the neighbors her son her own son—speak of the woman who died was killed had her throat slit. Some say she called them names. Others or even the same ones mention that she might have had a drinking problem at some point. But they can't be sure. Eulogy, words honoring a dead person, their sole eulogy. Even her son, her one child still alive, her son who lives across the street, had nothing else to say. But it had been years since she'd seen her son her daughter-in-law her grandchildren now all grown up. She didn't talk to them anymore, they didn't talk to her anymore. They saw each other on the street but they didn't wave, they didn't go over to each other. Not her grandchildren either, her grandchildren who had grown up who saw her also didn't wave to her anymore. They didn't come over when they saw her on the street with her cane, they felt no curiosity or pity, not even a reflex. That was their eightysomething grandmother and why should they care. It was at the trial that he—the man I'm talking about since he's the man on trial—saw them for the first time, her fiftysomething son her daughter-in-law her grandchildren. When all of them came feeling no shame about asking about the money yes no shame about being there at the trial for the money. Feeling no shame about never being there for her before. No shame about having nothing to share about her their mother or mother-in-law or grandmother. No shame about having no explanation, just, since they'd been asked all the same, that they'd gotten into an argument about errands. No shame about saying that he the son, the one son, got sick of running her errands. No shame about saying that they her daughter-in-law her grandchildren were all the same were all in agreement. And that since then they all saw her on the street almost every day because they lived practically across the street but they didn't wave to each other didn't talk to each other. No shame about being there for the damages for pain and suffering that the state always awards the family without burden of proof, it's covered by insurance. No shame about the law that has allowed them this.

It's for this reason, it's because the son got sick at some point of helping his mother, that he—the man I'm talking about since he's the man on trial—started running her errands two or three times a week. He came over to the old lady's place, she called him or even left him notes in his mailbox when she needed something. Apart from him and the building manager who did the shopping for her on Fridays at Franprix, her neighbors didn't do a thing. Some of them she'd asked but they'd straight up said no and when they were questioned, they just said that it wasn't their job to help her, they had to help themselves first. That's the sort of ugliness that comes out in a crime or a trial, the sort that's all around, from those being called witnesses, who didn't do a thing who'll never do a thing, who just stand around, next to them the perp is practically a saint.

The man who killed her was the only one to talk to her with any warmth, yes, let me speak of warmth. The man who killed her said that she was kind, that she had her moods it's true but not terrible, that with him she was cheerful, that she told him about her life, about her dead kids and her boy still alive who didn't come see her anymore, that she said she'd had enough of having to rely on others, said she wasn't long for this world, that she was living a nice quiet life, that he was rather fond of her. They couldn't stand hearing that, they told him to be quiet.

He killed the old lady the way he might have killed just anybody, the way he might have spat in just anybody's face. The way just any face deserves to be insulted to be spat on to be wrecked. There needs to be a sacrifice. For something unbearable to be purged. A man has to pay for all men. It doesn't solve anything because there's no solution but it has to happen, there's no getting around it, not for the one who kills not for the one who's been killed.

I killed the old lady but I could have killed just anybody the same way I would have spat in just anybody's face. Nobody's innocent. Every face reveals all humanity, the sum of all crimes. There needs to be an answer, there need to be consequences. There needs to be some act of violence or else nothing makes sense anymore. If you can't feel that deep down, if you can't see what I'm talking about, then you won't believe the way I do what that means: all of us.

He says his drugs got stolen. He says maybe it was his little brother, maybe his stepfather. Who knows, everybody lies, himself included. Holding a dealer's drugs is called being a drug nanny. Hashish sounds like the Eucharist, Take-this-all-of-you-and-eat-it, folks buy it folks take it sometimes they sell it. His mother his stepfather his brothers his wife his friends, everybody here or just about smokes. Dealer's math, eight hundred grams missing that's three thousand euros he's on the hook for. To him, three thousand euros **might** as well be a million. Workers of the world and the drug trade too. With a dealer there's no explaining, no apologizing, no negotiating. There's always a law. He was under pressure. He'd asked everyone, he'd asked his own parents since he was still a kid after all. His mother used her child benefits to help him. His father applied for a loan (not knowing why his kid needed money, not wanting to know why), the bank

(23)

turned it down, he wasn't in good shape, it's unwise to lend money to people about to die, *moritūrī tē salūtant* as it says in Suetonius. He'd tried to cook up schemes, robbing places, snatching purses, but the truth was he had no idea how to do that, the truth was that he was scared. The people who were supposed to help him let him down, it never worked. He told everyone about it, nobody could help him, he had to pay.

She can't bear to talk about it, you don't do that, snitch on a dealer to the cops, she just couldn't, but she wanted the police the judges to understand about her son, after all. Two heavies showed up, they came to her place, they grabbed her, took her for a drive in their car around the cité and then on the highway, without a word without a breath, taking her for a ride that's called. They took her for a ride then they drove her home. The dealer told her to pay up for her son if she didn't want him missing dead gone. He gave her a week. She said, these were her words, that she was a mother and she'd do what she had to for her son. The next day she'd withdrawn the money from her account. All she had, a thousand seven hundred euros, she gave him. After that, of course, there was the little detail that she had issues with direct debits not going through. A thousand seven hundred isn't three thousand. She couldn't pay the rest, she went to find the dealer, she pleaded with him. She told him she'd found some housecleaning work, he put her on a payment plan like a purchase from Darty, she gave him money every week. Now and then he'd show up at her place without any warning to keep up the pressure so she didn't forget. Took the mother for a ride around the cité and sent the little brother down to the cellar. When the little brother came back up he was pale as a ghost. He never said what happened. He never said a thing. He stayed in the apartment for three weeks and wouldn't come out. Wouldn't even go down to buy bread. The little brother wrote to child protective services after that. He wrote to social services to be sent to another home. He got an appointment for the 13th. They offered to put him in foster care in the Vendée.

He was supposed to leave with his wife and the little girl, that was the plan. He still had to pay four hundred and fifty euros, the remainder, the balance. He couldn't leave without paying. He couldn't leave and have his mother his brother stuck back there with the dealer. All he wanted was to be free to settle, words are funny that way. Stealing the purse taking the card withdrawing the money paying off his debt for drugs with the old lady's card, the old lady's pension, then leaving. Leaving for her city, the girlfriend the fiancée the wife he loved, the city by the sea with their baby, all three of them, finding work down there. She planned to clean houses, he needed to pass a test to be a waiter, they'd decided to move in with her mother first then find an apartment of their own once they had steady work. Leave his father his mother his brothers the dealer, leave the world of child benefits and drugs, the world of social workers judges and dealers. They even said they'd throw a going-away party.

Maybe he thought something was possible. If he found the money if he paid off his debt if he left this city if he settled by the sea if he got that far. If he managed to leave everything that had always been there. His father who wasn't his father, his little brother who was stealing his drugs, his mother and her meds and her hash, his mother who knew who his father was but who didn't want to tell him, his mother whom he shared joints with, his mother who had children in foster care but hadn't let him be placed even though he'd have liked that, even though that was the one thing that might have helped him, he was saying, his mother who reported him to the cops for iffy things, like his half sister getting molested, his mother accusing him before accusing his little brother, before her daughter was put in foster care, before his mother left his stepfather, before his stepfather wasn't allowed to see his daughter anymore, his mother who was also the only one to cover his ass when it came to the dealer, the only one to put up any money, the only one who came to see him in the slammer, to come to the trial, the only one to stick by him through thick and thin. And she was the one whom the dealer decided to strong-arm, the one he decided to take for a ride around the cité, his mother and not his father. His father who didn't know a thing who didn't want to know a single thing. Not that he wasn't his father not that his son wasn't going to class not that his son was smoking weed not that his son was a drug nanny not that his son was in a hole and had a dealer on his ass. His father like that monkey with hands over eyes hands over ears, his father who was always there too, putting him up, never asking questions, loving him without prying. His father who didn't know that he didn't know a thing, his father who was Ignorance and his mother who knew everything, who was Knowledge, good and evil together. Leave his father who wasn't his father, leave his mother, leave this whole mess. All he wanted was to get out. Get thee out of thy country, and from thy kindred, said the Eternal, but maybe there are people for whom that isn't possible.

These are small buildings that went up in the sixties fairly close to the apartment complexes from the same period. Well-maintained five-story structures painted white. Their entrances are in an alley parallel to the street serving as a parking lot for the renters, there are no owners these are public housing. Two highways run through the town, one to the west and one to the east, it has a RER station, several three-digit bus lines run nearby.

Ten stabs they told him. He hadn't counted, doing this sort of thing gets people in a state. It would be good to look into all the actions that get people into such a state that they stop thinking. Brain scientists might have made a list of them already. For his mother his brothers his wife his friends, it's hash or pills or booze or video games, things they're always getting told off about. Sex too maybe it's something so as not to think. People come up with words for that, talk about love or desire but maybe it's just something so as not to think. Something that crops up at the same age as hash by the way, at the same age as all the problems, all the ones that judges social workers pick up on, all the ones that get mixed together to make days, life, such a shitty thing. It's really something to see how the girls in the cité do it, how his friends do it, and how they all talk about it here. Something shitty, yes even when they're talking about love. Everyone's fooling everyone else, everyone's just cheating, that's how they learned to deal with it, you can't count on anyone if you're just trying to get by. PTSD is why he doesn't remember. That's what the brain scientists say, that it's just as bad for victims as for the perps, that the perps are just as able to be shocked, violence is traumatizing for them, their own violence. Not everyone likes that, not everyone likes that the perpetrators can be just like the victims, what the world wants is a wholly separate race of the guilty, it would be visible in their bodies and their souls, someone guilty wouldn't feel anything. What the world wants are guilty people who aren't like them at all, who make it clear to them that they aren't guilty, that's what the guilty are for. He does remember the stab to the throat, the one that made all the blood, the one that made it never-ending, that made him get it all over himself.

He went back to his place, he threw up, he read noon on the Freebox, he woke up his brother. Usually his brother, his little brother who was fifteen or sixteen who smoked and dealt, stayed with their mother but sometimes not. Sometimes he stayed with their father slept on a mattress in the living room. He shook him, he said Wake up, I need you, I killed the old lady. The little brother didn't ask questions. He saw the blood on the jacket the jeans the shoes, he said that he needed to get rid of those. They put the stained clothes in a plastic bag, they got dressed, they left. The little brother was wearing his Adidas LA

Trainers and he his Nike Air Max that a friend had given him, he had to toss the Nike Requins because of the blood. They walked downtown, they gave the bag of stained clothes and the old lady's bag to a Roma on a bike who was always going through the trash. The little brother left. He went to the ATM with the old lady's card. He withdrew the four hundred fifty euros, he called the dealer, he paid up. Then all he had to do was wait.

He did wait, he didn't flee, he waited. Three days until she was found, and then another three days until he was found. What else could he do. He stayed in the upstairs apartment belonging to his father where he lives with his girlfriend fiancée wife whom he loves, and the baby, the apartment that's exactly the same two-bedroom as the one belonging to the old lady directly downstairs, he slept in his bedroom that's directly above her bedroom, he crossed the living room right above the living room where she still was, where he was the only one to know that she lay in blood, the puddle of blood, throat open, he didn't move.

Did he think about the body, the rotting now beginning, it was getting warm too. Did he think about that, about her now a thing beginning to rot. Did he think about the flies on her eyes, her mouth, about the fly eggs in her body and the worms, about the green blotch on her belly, apparently it begins that way. Did he think about the old lady's body decomposing directly below his own living body. Or does a corpse stop being scary.

The building manager was surprised, it was Friday, she'd left for the weekend. But on Monday there was still no answer. The firefighters raised the ladder, broke a window, they saw her, they called the police. Law enforcement came, first local officers then municipal officers given the seriousness. Once the scene was fully secured and investigated, that's how they put it, the body was taken to the forensic-institute morgue for an autopsy. In the three subsequent days until his arrest, in the six days total following the murder, he stayed put he didn't move he answered questions he said he did like the old lady he agreed to a DNA swab he didn't leave he didn't flee he waited, what else was there for him to do.

Night protects criminals, night ends at 6 a.m. At six they came, the Paris cops given the seriousness of the crime. They hauled him off, they told him he had the right to remain silent, the right not to talk, they explained it. He remained silent. Then the car again, a judge for the arraignment and then another for placing him in custody. The protocol for locking someone in a cage. The fact that someone is locked in a cage is decided not by any single person, chosen not by any single person, but by multiple people, a totality of things for which no single person is responsible. People are locked up for nothing so when it's for something like killing nobody takes offense. A prosecutor two judges several policemen and gendarmes, the only surprise is how long it takes, the requisite wording. A court file number, a case number, a prisoner number, a cell number. The place of the prisoner of the accused of the one guilty of murder. A place, a longstanding place in the order of things.

Thou shalt not kill. Mother of all laws, bedrock of every moral system, of every contract, of every rule, of every code. No contract is truly ironclad. No law is truly rock-solid. Thou shalt not kill and why shalt thou not. There are so many people who knows what to do with them. Where to put them, how to feed them, keep them busy. Human life is like a sickness, an infection. Nothing admirable in principle. Nothing praiseworthy in practice. Do see how lives are put to use. How bodies and souls are treated, whether one's own or other people's. Just see what a man says, what he's like, just look, really look. Just see a man as he talks laughs gobbles fucks dies. How a man talks to his ilk, men women families, those who claim to love one another, those who love as they always say they do. Just see how ugly that is, men women the rich the poor, the horrors that reveals, that a man unleashes. Holy are those things, in principle and in practice, whether infinitely large or infinitely small, I don't see. The respect that would command, I don't see. Actually when looking properly I see the opposite.

So what difference does it make one old lady more or one old lady less, an old lady dying now or an old lady dying in two months. What does it matter how a man dies, a slow death or a single blow, by accident or by someone's hand, what does that change, what difference does that make—and for whom. In what way are such things holy. Holy they say not knowing what they mean. If it were holy existence wouldn't happen like this. If it were holy we wouldn't live the life we do. If life were holy it would be evident what men are obligated to do. Holiness would obligate all men all the time, if life were holy as men claim. Not considering their words.

No law is true, no principle, nothing is rock-solid. With every crime everything crumbles, all fake plaster. We are the pure, we are the saints, the last of the saints. Saints through demise if not through grace, saints unto crime, saints unto punishment. Against the unbearable that has to be borne, against all that is heinous and against indifference to that. Purity is only in affirming the impossibility, only in total defiance. Being the one to spit in the face of the world, to reject its lies, to lament its promises, to shriek that evil is the world itself. And to receive all the punishment as a baptism. Why not because everything is false. Yes, everything is false. And we are the other side of the lie. You know it. Of course you know it. It may be thanks to us that humanity still holds, we the little bastards full of hash killing old ladies in cités, we and our horde, we for all eternity. It may be thanks to us that there's still something true. That without us you would have nothing left. That without us you would fall like empty bodies. That if we didn't exist you would all start dying out. Expiring one by one of your ugliness that would come and eat you from the inside out. Your ugliness, all the rot of humanity, this white-hot rot in which you hold together. What way is there to live but in rot amid rotting, wondering what it means to exist, whether life really is holy and whether thou shalt not kill means something, something other than don't bother me in my own rot, in our respective rot in which we live we grow we die. Sometimes that's maddening, yes sometimes that's maddening. Let blood spew out at least. Let the horror come out. Blood rather than all the pus held in. Blood that lets us believe that not everything is a farce and that something is real.

Fleury-Mérogis Prison building D2 nine square meters for three. Toilets TV fridge hot plate, more like five square meters. He thought about animals. Smaller and smaller dogs, bigger and bigger cats, chowing down and sleeping, not hunting anymore, not biting anymore, never about to kill you. Only able to love animals now, tamer and tamer ones, less and less wild ones, men can only do that now. The Fleury rats and roaches that can be felt on one's face at night. Hardy animals those rats and roaches, animals that have existed for ages, that have survived everything, the last thing to die. Maybe what has no love will be the last thing to die.

There is a geography. We live in a vertical world, you don't see it. A world made up of worlds. Not adjoining but concentric, superimposed. Not unlike medieval depictions of the cosmos, not unlike Dante's circles of hell. Each world in contact only with those directly adjacent and no others. Prison is not equidistant from such worlds, is not an exoplanet, is rather a world at the edge of the last circle. A world that, for those at the bottom, is right there. And, for those at the top, far away really very far away. A world so far away for those at the top as to be unimaginable. To be believed the sole province of the monstrous, how could those at the top think otherwise. A world that you believe the sole province of the monstrous, how could you imagine otherwise. Vertical geography, yes, with you at the top. More or less on top by nature, there are gradations, but, wherever you are, if you are reading me then you are on top. The world on the bottom, the last of the worlds on the bottom, is the one with the trapdoor. No, not a trapdoor: wide-open double doors. Prisons are not the sole province of those who kill. No extraordinary act like killing is necessary, often it's an ordinary act that sets the wheels turning. An ordinary act in the world on the bottom. All it takes is turning a risk into a reality. Most activities in the world on the bottom carry risk. Capitalism, contrary to what it claims, does not reward risk. Accordingly, it off-loads risk. It off-loads risk to those who are losers before they are vanquished. The drug dealer off-loads risk to the drug nanny, just as the boss to the worker, the general to the private. The system off-loads risk to those for whom a loss will change nothing. Those on top do not know risk, they live in a world free of risk. Which paradoxically, for lack of courage, increases fear. The system favors an absence of risk, an absence of movement, the system wants exact replication, the working system wants to go on working as it always has. A working system is impossible to dismantle, men cannot do anything about it. Risk has nothing to do with evil. This is prison: when risk becomes reality. The risk that you have created. And that you have off-loaded on us. Even for your Saturday-night lines of coke and your Sunday joints the risk is us. You might go to rehab while we go to prison. Because that's all prison is, the place we go when we live in the world on the bottom and we fall off. If you fall off, you won't go to prison. You'll go live in a smaller apartment, you'll go work a job you're not as happy with, you'll go through problems, money problems, more or less, life problems, more or less, everyone's got their share, of course, and I'm not saying that you're safe from calamity. But you won't go to prison. You won't be sentenced by men in robes on the bench and you on the dock, you won't be handcuffed, you won't sleep in bedcovers smelling like piss, you won't be fed disgusting food, you won't have roaches in your bed and rats by your windows, you won't lose love, friends, a body against yours, or even your privacy. For that to happen you'd have to be born on the fringe. Have to have only ever known that fringe. This limbo of concrete and super-markets with streets named after poets only your sort care about. Yes, limbo. That's a real thing, limbo. Our world's full of limbo. Did you not know that? Prison is something that will never happen to you. It's a world too far from yours. It's the circle right below our own. The next town over. It's not another world. It's the world where those on the bottom are punished for all the world's sins. Sins you off-loaded on us, sins we commit for you. Sins we commit for a humanity that harbors all evil but that off-loads it onto people like me, like us, like all of us going to prison, because we're born for that, because we're born to serve you in every way possible, this included. Sins you live off of, that we commit and that you punish. Sins that are no more ours than yours, sins whose root, the reason of effects, lies not in those committing them but in all humanity.

I killed her but I killed her in your stead. I kill but I kill by you, for you, and with you. I kill because you feed off of my crime, because you feed off of assassins, I killed her to let you punish us, because this is the way of the world in need of endless victims, the world made up of executioners everywhere. There is no distinction (us all). You can judge me, sentence me, cast me aside, me and those like me, cast us even further aside, tell yourselves that evil is me, but evil is no less you than me. Thou shalt not kill, indeed. But not because thou art better than us, thou art not one bit better than us. For we must speak of good as that is the crux of this matter, good and evil, something you do have to confront, whether or not you are used to it now.

Not so tall, rather thin, very dark. Gypsy blood, bastard blood rising to the surface. His brothers used to say it showed they didn't share the same blood. He always dresses the same. He wears black Nikes jeans black tees a fake-leather jacket. He always has his cap on, the same one his little brother wears. The caps they had to burn after because of the camera on the ATM where he withdrew the old lady's money. He has a tongue piercing, missing upper-front teeth. He's asked to give his life story, he gives it biographical, factual.

The école named after a poet where a teacher slaps students. The collège named after a minister where conflicts between cités mean kids stick together with others from their own quartier. When he was twelve he made new friends, big kids three years older than him also from his quartier. The next year he starts tuning out, skipping class, hanging out with guys who finished earlier. He isn't held back. The year after that he stops going to class at all. He hangs around outside until school's out. He isn't held back. In the following year he's still not going to class at all. He's at the age where the French Republic isn't required to teach students like him. He doesn't move up a grade, he isn't going to lycée at all. He drops out of the school system entirely. He's sixteen, he's too young to work. About that time he becomes a father. He says that he had social workers keeping an eye on him, a juvenile-court judge, he doesn't remember their names. What else, they ask him. Well he'd have liked to be a soccer player, he was in two or three big games, he was supposed to do tryouts, he got an infection because of his kidneys, they weren't able to take him. And he'd have liked to be in foster care too. They offered him a placement in a fancy country home. He was fourteen, he wanted to do it. That was when he wasn't going to school anymore, when he was skipping all his classes, the age when it could have worked out well for him the way it did for his big brother. His mother said there were problems with the damp, that it was bad for his kidneys, she said no.

He says I have a father and a mother, two brothers, one older one younger. And two half sisters. The one my father had before he met my mother and whom I don't really know. The other that my mother had with her new guy and who was put in foster care. He doesn't know how old she is. Eight or ten. She's with a foster family because of the molesting, that's when his mother changed her daughter, his sister's diapers, and saw that her skin was irritated, that was the accusation his mother made against him. He says nothing came of the investigation. He doesn't know maybe that's why his sister was put in foster care, he probably doesn't know either that his stepfather, the father of his half sister, isn't allowed to see his daughter anymore. That that's the reason, because of that whole thing, that his mother left his stepfather. It's the mother who says all that. Not at the hearing, not in front of everyone, but in the judge's chambers. She says it's a bit murky, she says she can't go into all the details, she's embarrassed, maybe she feels ashamed. He says he was really angry at his mother, that he's forgiven her now. He says that the only one to always believe in him is his father, his father who isn't his father.

He has an older brother. An older brother who got out. The minute the parents got divorced the minute everything started to go bad he was gone. That big brother did what was best, he cleared out, at fourteen, of his own will. He never came back. Now he's baccalaureate level, he's over eighteen, he works, he even has an apartment. His job's stocking shelves at a Leclerc from midnight to 4 a.m.

He also has cousins on his mother's side in Portugal but he doesn't know them. He had a grandmother down there, he must have seen her three or four times, he doesn't remember. His grandparents on his father's side are dead. His father has a photo that he keeps in his closet.

His father is a sanitation worker. He's sick but he's still on a contract. He still has a salary. His mother was a waitress. That's how they met. At a bar in Paris in the nineteenth arrondissement where she worked and where he went after work, the nineteenth was his route. She stopped. Now she lives on welfare benefits.

They split up when he was in sixth grade. He stayed with his mother first. Then there were fights. Then she accused him of molesting his little sister. Before accusing his brother. Before the girl was put in foster care. She kicked him out because of that or because she was tired of him living there with his girlfriend fiancée wife whom he loves. His mother kicked them out. They went to live with his father, where their daughter was born. His father who believed him about the molesting. His father who'd always believed him. His father who wasn't his father but who'd always believed in him. That was two or three years ago now. He says that he's close with the old man because he always believed in him. Sometimes he brought the little girl along to pick him up from work.

It's when they started drifting apart that things began to go downhill. He overheard that he wasn't his father's son, his big brother left, their mother began smoking, taking all those meds, getting bogged down in depression, getting stuck in everything. That's when he and then his brother stopped going to school. They all began smoking, hanging around, not knowing what to do with themselves. He was ten, maybe eleven or twelve. It can be too late all too soon, too late not to be a drug nanny, too late not to be a dropout, too late not to be a teen dad, too late not to have a dealer on his ass and a debt to pay off, too late to wonder what to make of himself.

He started smoking cigarettes at thirteen, joints at fourteen. He never stopped. He tokes up in the morning when he wakes up, then in the afternoon and the evening, five or six joints a day, he says. His wife smokes hash too. His mother too. His little brother too. His stepfather too. His friends too. Only his dad doesn't smoke. Apparently stopped drinking too, because of his heart problems. His big brother doesn't smoke either. The two brothers don't see each other much. He buys the hash with welfare benefits. He sells a bit too and that covers costs. His mother says he gets her drugs for her. That's on my little brother since I moved out, he says. Whenever he stops by, she asks him to roll her a joint. The judge asks him if he thinks that's odd, he's polite, he says yes.

He says he isn't close with anyone. The old lady wasn't close with anyone either.

At night he smokes, he plays online, the goal is survival he finishes every level. He wins the game, he goes to bed late, he gets up early. Around seven he does the first bottle feeding, he changes his daughter's diaper, his wife gets up, he goes back to bed. He gets up in the afternoon around two or three, they usually skip lunch, he smokes a joint, he logs into some game, he and his friends meet up there, they make plans for later in the cité or at the stadium, on the Astroturf. He goes for a walk with his wife and their baby, they go run errands, sometimes they pay with their own money, their welfare-benefits check for a family of three is seven hundred and twelve euros, sometimes it's with his father's money. His father doesn't mind pitching in, he says that's how it's done. He does still get riled up sometimes seeing them not working, but it's not for lack of trying, they've tried, of course they have. They tried whenever they went somewhere, whenever they were someplace else. They tried in Alsace when they went to stay with her family, they tried in Bayonne where she also had some family, they dropped off résumés at McDonald's, at restaurants. They were still minors at the time, nobody wanted them, nothing worked out. There was that thing in Nantes, that could have worked out, could that have worked out, what did it matter to wonder.

He's an unexceptional person. It's the psychiatrist who says so, an educated man, a scientist of the human soul. He came to see him at Fleury one afternoon, they talked for an hour or two, the psychologist put together his report. His expert report, an expert on what is exceptional and what is unexceptional. It's unclear what's meant by this "unexceptional," if that's in terms of his life or of the murder. Maybe it's the act itself that's unexceptional. Maybe even killing someone by stabbing them ten times is unexceptional. Yes, maybe even killing does nothing, changes nothing, carries no more meaning than any other act in one's life. The report was introduced into evidence during the trial so the jurors could know whom they were judging, the reason they'd been brought here, the matter they'd been summoned for. So they could see how the murder was unexceptional, how the trial was unexceptional, how their verdict was unexceptional, how the perpetrator was unexceptional, how the old lady was unexceptional, how they themselves were unexceptional. How everything was unexceptional.

She was born down in the city by the sea, down there is where she grew up. Her mother was the one to raise her. Her father lives in a trailer on a campsite, he's a Traveler she says. They met on Skyrock, they started talking on MSN Messenger. Both of them fifteen years old, then. Like Romeo and Juliet. She'd stopped going to school too. She had a Gypsy father too. She was a foster child too. She was living with her mother too. Her mother who drank the way his mother smoked. Her mother who was a cleaning woman just like his father was a sanitation worker. Other people's filth making jobs for them. First they texted then they called each other then he went to see her in the city by the sea. He stayed for two weeks, she came back with him. He told her that his parents had died in a car accident in Portugal, he said that his mother and father were just his aunt and uncle. It was a lie but not far from the truth, only half true. Things started off well, then there were arguments. His mother kicked them out, they went to live with his father. There was the investigation, she had the baby.

She'd had flings of her own. He had, too, if not as many. He talked about some girlfriend whom his little brother stole. She talked about some boyfriends who were serious and some who weren't so much. She was with one for two years. They both said the same thing: they met and they'd been together ever since.

He picked the baby's name, she said Fine. It was a bit soon of course but what mattered was having a kid. She's usually the one looking after their kid but not always. He says We play together. I'm the one scolding her too. I'm the one setting limits. She'll be three in September. She has tantrums at times of course but she listens. I know how to take care of her.

When it comes to the girlfriend fiancée wife whom he loves, he says that he tells her everything, that she's the only one he talks to, he says that when it comes to him she knows everything.

She didn't come see him, she didn't bring their daughter to the visiting room, she's with another guy now. When he calls it's the other guy who answers, he tells him not to call again. His replacement snitched on him to the jail. There was a search, they found the cell phone, he was put in solitary. Two weeks in confinement, two weeks alone, without any walks, any TV, any visitors. He's not seeing his daughter again; by the time he gets out she'll be an adult.

Don't think he's calling himself innocent. Don't think he's calling himself a victim. Don't think he's absolving himself. Yes, he's guilty. He's guilty of giving in, he's guilty of not letting himself be crushed. He's guilty of being unreasonable, he's guilty of not staying in his lane, the lane he belongs in. Of upsetting the order of things. He's guilty of falling. He's guilty of having chosen downfall rather than paralysis. Because everything is decided in advance. There are the losers and the winners and it has been decreed long in advance. Everything is determined before the act, what's to be done about that, nothing. He has signed his own death warrant by believing, however briefly, that he could have escaped. Escaped what amounts to the cité, his family, the dealers. The sin of hubris. Ulysses's sin too but Ulysses was king of Ithaca. He is unhappy like Gwynplaine, the Man Who Laughs Before the House of Lords, but while Gwynplaine may be a bastard he is also a lord. He is guilty of having believed whereas men like him ought not to believe anything. For there is nothing to believe. He is guilty, yes, but he is guilty in our stead. Because someone has to bear the cross. Because someone has to bear the burden.

I sign my own death warrant by believing, however briefly, that I could have escaped. For having believed whereas people like us ought not to believe anything. For there is nothing to believe. I am guilty, yes, but I am guilty in your stead. Because someone has to bear the cross, because someone has to bear the burden.

Ignominy in and of itself. And of his own doing rather than that of others. Ignominy as banner why not. I who am writing this book am paying homage, through this book and my others, to negative qualities. He is the facts. I am the one talking. Everything is true. Everything. Him me you. (I am writing the life of the saints.)

Maybe becoming a murderer is what it takes to have the right to be a bastard. A bastard, yes, but what does it matter in the end. Having an answer as to who one is or isn't. Or about what is. Because the question is never who one is but what is. The question is the world, it's us all, always, and the lies all around.

He was asking the question and there was no answer. The only question he ever asked, never stopped asking, and nobody gave him an answer. There's no answer, the young narrator is told at the start of Remembrance of Things Past. And for him too, yes, don't laugh, for him as much as for Proust, because it's always about us all, he's told There's no answer. Bastard, his brothers and his father's family always told him. Bastard, his father said of him to his mother when he left. An argument he overheard as they were getting divorced when he was starting to hang out, he was ten maybe eleven, starting to skip class. That he was a bastard, that he wasn't his father's son, the father who was leaving because he wasn't his son. What he wanted was to know. One only leaves innocence through sin, one only leaves innocence through downfall, everyone knows this, that everything always starts through a crime. He asked them, he asked his father to take a DNA test, his father said no, he said it was too expensive, he asked his mother, who lied to him like usual. It took killing the old lady, the police taking DNA samples of all the building's inhabitants to compare to what was found in the old lady's apartment on the knife he left on the table, the bent blade sticky with blood with his fingerprints and all, when he finally got up. It took a murder for a free DNA test. It took all that for him to be told that he was both a murderer and a bastard. He wanted to know and once he did, he cried.

He's the bastard, an only child of sorts. Like Him, yes, the one you're thinking of. He sought out his biological father but his mother never wanted to give him his name. He is the son of the one who has no name. Of the one who cannot be named. Yes, like the one you're thinking of. He bears the name of his brothers' father, of the one who recognized him, who raised him. He says that his brothers always held it against him, that they always talked about this difference, a flaw is also a privilege. After his parents got married, after the oldest brother was born, there were arguments. His mother said that his father was a drunkard, that he was a wifebeater, she got out. She spent some time with her family in Portugal. She had a lover, a fling with a Gypsy. And then they reconciled, she came back, she told him she was pregnant, he said That baby's my son. He had a falling out with his sister over that, his sister who said this son wasn't his. A few years later the youngest son was born. There were three brothers. But there was always this matter of bastardy. Everyone talked about it but the facts were never clear. It was always there, in the background, something that couldn't be nailed down, that was always slipping away, that he couldn't escape.

He killed her, that woman, but it could have been anyone.

It's the big brother. He works. The only one in his family who does. He stocks shelves at a Leclerc at night. Between midnight and 4 a.m. See, escape is possible. He just rented an apartment in another banlieue, a better banlieue, near his job. He left his family, he'd been in foster care, he wanted that. He made it all the way to *terminale* to get a professional baccalaureate in retail, he doesn't have his baccalaureate he's just reached the baccalaureate level. He doesn't have a history with the police or the courts. He's been a victim. At nine or ten years old he was beaten with brass knuckles. He had to get an operation, he was in and out of the hospital, even now his doctor still keeps an eye on him. He says that beating and his parents' divorce changed everything in the family. It was a normal family before. After the divorce his two brothers fell in with the boys from the cité, their mother stopped working. He wanted to leave.

That's why he was put in foster care and never came back. He's on good terms with his parents. He says he's better off the less he sees his brothers.

It's the little brother. He's sixteen. Doesn't go to school anymore. He smokes and deals drugs. He's been in foster care already, three places now. He was fourteen the first time and it was his idea, he wanted to get away. Then he came back. Now with everything happening he wants to leave again. Maybe this—the old lady's murder and his brother in prison—will save him. Maybe that'll be one good thing to come of this. Maybe being in foster care still won't help him any.

It's the old lady's son. He's a delivery driver. Grew up here. His brother's dead, his sister too, both his parents now. He's married, he lives with his wife, they have three children. His daughter works at the town hall, one of his sons in an auto shop, the youngest is still with them. He owns a Renault, he doesn't own any real estate. He has an email address but he can't remember it. He doesn't have a history with the police or the courts. He saw his mother the day before the murder, she was walking down the street with her cane and a shopping bag, she was wearing brown jogging pants and a coat, it was noon or half past noon, he was going home for lunch, he didn't wave to her. He was on the way to work when he got the call, he was filling up the tank at the Total gas station when he answered his phone. He had no idea what his mother must have been thinking. My poor little maman, he says, She didn't have a big pension.

It's the dealer. He's in a suit and they all, the judges and even the cops, call him monsieur. He has a national identity card, a driver's license, he owns a Renault Laguna. He's registered in the social-security system, he isn't on government benefits. He says he doesn't have a cell phone number. He testifies that he works off and on with a friend in a sandwich truck. He has a history with the police and the courts. There are ten charges on his criminal record. He's been in prison three times. He was born in Paris, in the tenth arrondissement. He grew up in the same town as those in question here, still lives there. He acknowledges that he is being questioned in the context of the investigation into the death of the old lady found dead in connection with criminal activity on … to … in any case on national territory and within the statute of limitations. He has been summoned as a witness. That's emphasized. Witness, not suspect. He's not here to be charged in connection with his business matters or how he manages them. He's not being charged in connection with anything. They thank him for coming. For having made time for them, as a busy man. They just want him to confirm this debt, the motive for the crime, the crime for which they already have an alleged perpetrator. There is only one guilty man, the one they're holding in custody. A trial is a straightforward matter and should stay so. They call him monsieur. He confirms the facts and the amount, three thousand euros and four hundred fifty. Didn't he go a bit too far when it came to recovering his debt, he smiles, of course not. Everyone smiles back, Thank you monsieur they say.

It's the father. He says that he was born here. That his parents were born here. He's always lived here. His parents too. His brother and his sister live close by. His oldest daughter who works in the civil service too, his daughter from a previous marriage, he doesn't see her often she's busy but they talk on the phone. He's been working since he was sixteen. His sister got him in at Nord-Transport then in the eighties he was hired by the Paris city government as a machine operator. With his illness he stopped driving. When he was still working, what he did was distribute shovels and brooms to his colleagues. He had an operation he spent six months in the hospital. That was when everything happened with the dealer. That was when his son asked him to apply for a loan to help pay off something he didn't know about, in any case the bank turned him down. As for his job he's waiting to be cleared by his doctors. He's working part-time for health reasons at the moment. He took in his son when his mother kicked him out, him and his fiancée, the baby was born while they were staying with him. They ask him if he knows, he says yes he knows everyone in his family smokes weed, the two younger sons and his ex-wife, they ask him what he thinks, he says he doesn't like it but that's just how things are. He used to smoke cigarettes, he's quit almost completely since the operation. Regarding his paternity, he says he didn't want to know, now that he does it doesn't change anything.

It's the mother. She was born in Brazil. Grew up in Portugal. She came to France at eighteen to work. Cafés, bars, temp jobs. She stopped working many years ago, she lives on welfare benefits. She settled here twenty-five years ago with her husband, the sons' father, she's lived in the same apartment since. She still has her mother in Portugal, she doesn't see her often. She's sick, her kidneys her ears, just like her son. She has bouts of depression. As for the weed she'd like to kick the habit. She says that when the cops told her that her son was a murderer she didn't feel well. She says I know it has nothing to do with his father not being his father but still. She thinks she didn't do everything right as a mother. She's single. She left her baby daughter's father because of the whole thing around the kid. Her daughter in a foster home she goes to see every so often.

It's the friends. The ones he hangs around with, the closest ones, the little gang of three or four, and then the others. They met in collège. They do or do not have a history with the police. They work or don't work. They often live with their parents. They're the ones he hangs out with at the stadium or elsewhere in the cité. They don't go to cafés, bars, nightclubs, movie theaters, they don't go on vacation together, they meet up on the street. What they do is they sit down, they smoke, they talk.

There's the one who's like a brother to him and who's also a father of a two-year-old girl. He's the one who looks after her since his girlfriend left, he has custody of her. He lives with his mother he doesn't have a job he has a history with the police for use and possession. They see each other with their girls almost every afternoon. They sit down and they smoke, he says. He's the one who gave him the black cap with the metallic brand logo.

There's the one who's a municipal officer. Has a history with the police. He testifies You could say we grew up together, we see each other at the Towers or at the stadium, we talk about everything and nothing, we just sit, we smoke a little joint, we don't see each other as often since he has a baby a wife, we still see each other though.

There's the one who lives with his parents, who's out of work, who says he almost never goes out. He testifies that he isn't interested in getting involved in all this. He acknowledges that he smokes a bit but what he wants is to get out of here.

There's the one doing his apprenticeship at a bakery. He got fired. He's looking for a new boss for the fall. He lives with his parents along with his brother and his two sisters. He has a history with the police of shoplifting.

There's the one who's a child-center counselor for the city. Has a history with the police he doesn't say why. Provides the same descriptions as the others.

There's the one just out of prison. Nine months at Fleury. He's older, they knew each other before. About the guy in question here he says An acquaintance, not a friend, we smoked together, good to see you good to see you. He says that he's a kid from the cité.

Us all. The old lady who was born close by, my father who was born here, my mother who isn't going anywhere, my brothers, my friends who were all born here, the dealer who grew up with us, the old lady's son who lives across the street, her grandson who lives two streets over, her granddaughter who works at City Hall, the neighbors, the building manager who's been there for thirty-three years. Just people from around here. People who've lived here forever. Since the sixties, since the eighties, since when the public-housing complexes went up or the four-story cités. People who came here shortly before or shortly after. People like me who were born of those people. People around here often for several generations. People from around here who are born here who settle here who die here. Low-skilled workers or unemployed folks, young old, poor or half poor. Us all. With or without records, with or without jobs, with or without hash, with or without child benefits or welfare. We get out when we can but it's not often that we can.

Those who leave go to another banlieue. That's what the perfect brother did, the one who works, the one the judges like, when there's a will there's a way. Stocking shelves, sorting goods at night under fluorescent lights. From wholesale distribution for wholesale consumption. Which makes billionaires off the backs of the poor. Which rots bodies souls landscapes through terrible food and ugliness, which takes the money of those who don't have any. He hangs in there he doesn't complain. You have to understand the hate and disgust needed to stick through years in foster care rather than grow up at home, to stick through lycée without anyone to tell him how things work, to fail the baccalaureate of course but be able to say baccalaureate level, to stick around in jobs, internships, temporary contracts, permanent contracts. The hate and disgust of everything else to cling to this, be proud of it. His brothers, his family disgust him, their life disgusts him, the ins and outs of hash and of dealing disgust him, that his brother will end up in prison or with a bullet to the head has always been obvious to him, he said as much to their mother, he has every reason to stock shelves under fluorescent lights at night.

Us all, perfect little angels, playing our roles, working when we can, picking up your trash cleaning your offices or stocking your store shelves, buying your products, filling your prisons, justifying your laws, bent double, the law of the market or the law of legal codes doesn't matter. When are you giving us a round of applause.

Us all means you too. I'm telling you what you don't want to see in yourselves. Your lives are no worthier than ours. Your money your comfort your culture your work your loves are worthless. Your bigger apartments your nicer cities harbor the same crumbling walls, your perfumed skin the same rot. There are only scared selves, shocked sleepwalkers. Lives clinging willy-nilly to anything to anyone, to the first oncomer to the first offer. The stories we tell ourselves, oh all the stories. Of damned souls clinging to one another without ever making a choice. You know this. Of course you know this. Your unshakable urge to get away from us is all in vain. Our poverty and our despair are the same as yours. You are lost, perhaps far more than we are. Caught in your own lies you sink with each day into deeper madness. All your wealth spent on yourself, plumbed to keep you as you are, is no longer just a sin it's now a sickness.

Your shrinks whom you paid in cash to clear your consciences clear nothing. Your always-healthier food washes away nothing. You are the darkness. What we are is you but with less flab, you but with less fear, less falsity, less foulness, we are existence as close as possible to what it is to be a man. Humanity, do you ever think about that? What humanity is, what humanity demands of us? Does humanity, all that is lost and that despairs of being saved, still exist for you, has it ever existed? Our limbo is the center of the world. It is where humanity is now. We are the damned and we the saints. And maybe, just as it's too late for me, it's too late for you too.

The night before his arrest, a Tuesday, he threw a party. He invited his friends for whiskey and joints at the stadium where they always met up. His last round before parting ways. Before leaving for the city by the sea he was saying. Before getting arrested. There were ten of them, a dozen maybe. His friends, his wife and his daughter, his friends' girlfriends. He went to the barber's first. To look good. The shaved neck of convicts. He passed around some Ballantine's. He bought a bottle and some cigarettes—or one of his friends did because he didn't have any money. They passed around joints. He had on black jeans and Air Maxes. For the reasons we're already familiar with he didn't have his Requins or the black cap anymore, that surprised the guests. By eight everyone was headed home. There were kids to put to sleep. His last supper.

He's in a dock on the right, a bulletproof glass cage. He has on a black Nike tracksuit. There are two gendarmes behind him, this is the procedure. On the other side of the glass, the back of his lawyer, the black robe. On the bench, seated behind a long table, the judges are as judges always are: at center, on high, in majesty. In the middle the presiding judge in red and black then two judges in black and the jurors come as they are. Nine people in all, there had been twelve, and then they were culled. Beside the actual judges, the ones there to sentence, is the public prosecutor. He too is elevated and outfitted in a large black and red robe in white-ermine trim with black spots like the kings of a thousand years ago. Nothing has changed since Joan of Arc. Still the same masquerade, the same costumes, the same unholy Mass. That's the first thing you see, before everything begins, that trials are a sham, that the law is a farce. He thinks that everything is the wrong way around. He thinks that the judges ought to judge him from ground level, without robes and ermine trim, in a tracksuit like his own. He thinks that it's he who ought to be on high above them on the bench, in a red robe with fur trim. Aesthetically speaking, that's how he sees it. The state should do its punishing on its knees. And being punished should be nigh on an honor. Yes let him speak of honor, it feels like that's what's missing.

He's allowed to have an opinion. It's his trial, after all, not everyone gets one. And it's not all that often that people take such interest in him, and in such pomp and ceremony. It's an event practically a privilege. You can look at it that way. Then he thinks that he can expect something of this. Something for him. Something that's not contempt. Their contempt for him and inevitably his contempt for them. Inevitably yes, given how they operate. They're not serious, that's what stands out to him, the lack of seriousness that ruins it all. It's as if they didn't understand that he's the first one to want to be judged, that it's he first and foremost who wants that from their justice, who's only ever wanted that.

But justice doesn't care, that's not what it's there for.

It's a simple case, the trial won't take long. Three days. The minimum for criminal court. Two days for arguments one day or just a few hours for deliberations. For a hundred and fifty euros on average per day the jurors are paid what he got in killing the old lady. Four hundred and fifty euros: what he and she are worth.

The law nothing but the law, the French Republic is secular, this isn't America. No Bible to swear on, people swear but they swear on nothing. Nothing that tells those judging that they too might be judged one day, that they too are guilty of their faults, that nobody escapes judgment. Nothing that recalls the story of that guy who was poor the way he is poor, who was judged the way he is being judged, and who was God for that. It's done and dusted with those stories. The state is modern, justice is profane, justice is human, it sees itself as human. All that remains is this vulgar parody, that of its functionaries in priests' robes.

Down below the witnesses the cops the dealer the expert psychiatrist come to the stand, turning their backs on him, ordered around like children by the men in red above them. How could they not do what is asked of them, paint him as a murderer. Every so often his lawyer stands up, attempts something. They almost seem mad at him for defending him. His trial goes by. He gets bored.

He kills for four hundred fifty euros. That was what the papers said. As if a million would be any more understandable. As if a million would have been forgivable. "Paltry motive," the prosecutor says likewise. "Trifling amount," rages this functionary in a red medieval costume who's gotten paid every month since he won a competitive exam at twenty-one years old. An exam designed for people like him, who went to lycée, guys who would never have got put in foster care, who would never have skipped classes and still moved up to the next grade each year because nobody cared, until the system spat them out, because the system doesn't even try for the ones on the bottom, guys who don't roll joints for their mother when they're thirteen, who aren't accused by their mother of molesting their baby sister because their mother would rather blame a twelve-year-old son than a brand-new husband, people who don't know what it's like when a dealer is unhappy, who don't know what it's like to get beaten up in a basement, who don't know what it's like to be all alone in the world, where the police aren't whom you call when you get beaten up, where when you get beaten up you just shut your mouth, where when you get threats you just shut your mouth, where the police are the ones to interrogate you about your little sister because of accusations your mother made, where money doesn't come from the Ministry of Justice but from the dealer. That's the sort of guy the prosecutor is, a guy who gets paid every month of his life because many years ago he gave three good answers to teachers and who gets outraged at paltry motives and trifling amounts. A guy who doesn't know what fear can be like, who doesn't know how evil comes in, how it just slips in little by little, that it always comes through lack of money, lack of money and lack of love because love isn't possible when there's no money or that it's not the same thing, that it's always dirtied by all the rest, by everything that's ruined, a guy who must talk about literature, have a nice collection of books, take trips, show his children Rome, a guy who has political opinions, who knows what justice is, it's his job, his specialty, he went to university for that, a guy who's never experienced injustice, who can't even imagine it. That's what's needed of judges like him, specially chosen not to know what injustice is, what lack of money is, shitty lives, everything's set up for that, otherwise they couldn't judge, otherwise there wouldn't be justice.

Even if the matter bears his name, what plays out has nothing to do with him. He stays quiet and they talk. It's insane how they talk. That's what he thinks he who stays quiet and who gets judged. That's what he sees all of a sudden, their mania. They talk like madmen, as if they'd fall apart if they didn't talk, if for one second they stopped, men who could sink into a hole, a silence, into the prospect of the other person's words, so they talk talk talk, not seeing not looking not listening, hunched over, blind, pathetic.

Maybe this madness of speech warrants some consideration. The madness that plays out in a courtroom, in every trial, the madness that's everywhere. This mania for filling silence. This zeal to judge, everything and everyone. This obsession with endlessly explaining how others are wrong. Who are you hoping to convince beside yourselves. Who are your closing speeches, your pleas meant for. Maybe this justice only serves you. Maybe you're just talking to yourselves when you judge us. Maybe this justice is just an incantation for your laws, just to affirm that your goodness exists and that goodness is you because evil is us, just to reassure yourselves. Against whatever void within yourselves you're battling.

You're sick men. Sick with your empty lives. Sick with your off-loaded cruelty. Sick with your lies. Sick with your betrayal. With the great betrayal of your principles. You are traitors to yourselves. You can always work yourselves up, always talk more and always talk louder, I the guilty, I the murderer, I pity you.

Only once the sentence was handed down did he realize the extent of their innocence. Were it not so great they would not have been able to do what they did. They were the Happy, the Just, he envied them. Because evil to them was him, and it was good that forced them to sentence him. Through his crime he enabled them to believe in good, he showed them that evil exists. Through their sentencing they showed him that they didn't see what they were doing, that they didn't see what they were saying, that their good or their evil resided not in acts but in other things, very small things, like one's position in a courtroom, like the moment when the hits start being counted, the ones before and the ones after being nothing, nothing other than causes or consequences, innocent, of the act that society would ask them to judge. He envied them. He envied them for still not knowing that all was lost and nothing mattered. For still having sidestepped that moment in which it becomes clear that there's nothing to be done. That the game is rigged, fixed from the start. That good and evil do not exist. Which amounts to saying that evil swallows up all good. Yes he envied them their innocence.

He loved them for enabling him to bear all the evil. All his and that of others. That of his family, the dealer, his wife who'd cleared off, his daughter who would learn to hate him, his mother who'd accused him of committing pedophilia on his sister to cover up for his stepfather, his father who didn't show up to his trial, his brother who'd stolen his hash, the old lady who didn't give two shits about anyone anymore, the old lady's children who'd never given two shits about her, the evil of this republic in the name of which he was being judged, the evil of the law saying that they were all equal, the evil of the jurors whom the state paid to sentence him, the evil of this whole parade of good on the bench, of all these priests of goodness in their blood-red robes proceeding to the sacrifice, of all the good above him, the way good had always been in his life, inaccessible, irretrievable, him in the glass cage as deep down he had always been, with the two polite gendarmes, him the animal comforting them with the idea that this is no man, that men were people like them, people who can do all the evil they'd like so long as they don't kill anyone, but really all the evil yes and that's called good, and on that basis they judged him, on that basis all the men who ended up one day like him in a cage were judged, because progress changes nothing and it's needed every so often, for men to kill other men, some going down a street, going through their wretched lives, so that others later do so in the name of goodness, from on a bench, from on high, to make good exist, for this Mass that revives as a blood-letting purges bad blood.

For every heaven a hell. For your heaven to exist there has to be a hell beneath it, our hell. That's how things work. You live off of our damnation. The law is that. The law is the dividing line between heaven and hell, put purgatory wherever you like. Our stories of deals, and being foster children, and school that doesn't matter, and our cookie-cutter apartments, and our ugly cities, and all the violence, and police custody, and prison, and our pathetic lives, it has to be possible to calculate how many poor people it takes for one rich person. For one normal life, how many prisoners, how many guys on meds and on benefits. How many below the poverty line for how many above. How many guys in psych wards. How many forevers like our own for an hour of your lives. One hour with a woman who loves you. One hour with your well-behaved children. One hour in a city that isn't ugly. On a café terrace. One hour with your books. One hour working because your work raises you up while ours brings us down.

You are not so naive as not to see, as not to know how things work. I don't think you're naive. I think you know quite well that you're feeding off of us. That your morals hide your faults. That your laws hide your crimes. That your good your beauty your justness hide your violence and our servitude. We're the ones making your heaven. Yes us, the ones on the bottom, the ones in the basements, in the banlieues, in the outskirts, in the no-man's-lands. For people like you how many guys like us. Maybe there's a ratio in the order of the world, a secret balance between happiness and unhappiness, wealth and poverty, the vanquishers and the vanquished, the happy and the desperate, those who can live out drama and those who can only suffer tragedy. Yes maybe that's the Faustian bargain, but not between you and yourself, the Faustian bargain with you on one side and us on the other. You know perfectly well that's how things work. That we'll always be in our place, on the bottom, that if there is no below there is no above. I wonder if there's a mathematical law. I wonder if there's a magical number, like that castle of the Knights Templar with its eight towers and eight sides all built around the number eight which is the symbol of infinity. Maybe your world, too, your world of law, of liberty, of progress, and of culture, is built around a secret number, and this number is that of evil. This world of equality and justice, this world of delicacy and good taste, this world of intelligence and books, your world that will never be our own, that above the one in which we live, that which feeds on ours. You did right to reject God, to cancel the final judgment, to stop fearing the hour at which you might be judged on all the evil on which is built your good.